DATE DUE			
MAR 8 '94			
DEC 4 '01			
NOV 18			
5-18-07			

Doodle Flute

written and illustrated by
Daniel Pinkwater

Macmillan Publishing Company
New York

Collier Macmillan Canada   Toronto

Maxwell Macmillan International Publishing Group
New York   Oxford   Singapore   Sydney

Macmillan Publishing Company
866 Third Avenue, New York, NY 10022
Collier Macmillan Canada, Inc.
1200 Eglinton Avenue East, Suite 200, Don Mills, Ontario M3C 3N1
First edition   Printed in Singapore

10   9   8   7   6   5   4   3   2   1

The text of this book is set in 14 point Usherwood Book.
The illustrations are rendered in color markers on paper.

Library of Congress Cataloging-in-Publication Data
Pinkwater, Daniel Manus, date.
Doodle flute / written and illustrated by Daniel Pinkwater. — 1st ed.
p.   cm.
Summary: Relates how Kevin Spoon acquired a doodle flute and made a friend.
ISBN 0-02-774635-6
[1. Flute—Fiction.   2. Friendship—Fiction.]   I. Title.
PZ7.P6335Do   1991   [E]—dc20   90-6622   CIP   AC

To Jill, again

Kevin Spoon had a nice life.

He had nice parents.

He had a nice house.

He had his own room.

He had his own bathroom.

He had his own TV.

He had his own VCR.

He had his own stereo.

He had his own computer.

He had a ten-speed bike.

He had professional running shoes.

He had a professional first baseman's glove.

He had purebred guppies.

He had a waterproof watch.

His clothes were nice.

He had pizza every day.

Kevin Spoon was a lucky kid.

His mother and father said so.

And he thought so.

In back of Kevin Spoon's house was the yard.

In the yard was the pool.

Behind the pool was the fence.

Beyond the fence was the alley.

One day, Kevin Spoon was sitting on the fence.

Someone came down the alley.

It was Mason Mintz.

A weird kid.

Mason Mintz lived up the street.

He always looked sloppy.

He wore cheap sneakers.

He had a plaid hat.

He always wore it.

Mason Mintz and his mother and father planted stuff in their back yard.

They grew pumpkins.

Mason Mintz saw Kevin Spoon.

"Ho, Kevin," he said.

"What do you mean, 'Ho,'?" Kevin Spoon said. "You're supposed to say 'Hi.'"

"Why?" Mason Mintz asked.

"Because that's what you say," Kevin Spoon said. "Nobody says, 'Ho.'"

"I say it," Mason Mintz said.

"Why?"

"I like the way it sounds," Mason Mintz said.

"You're not normal," Kevin Spoon said.

"Maybe not," Mason Mintz said. "Do you want to see my doodle flute?"

"What is that?" Kevin Spoon asked.

"It is this," Mason Mintz said. He took something out of his back pocket.

It looked dumb.

"It looks dumb," Kevin Spoon said.

"Listen to this," Mason Mintz said.

He blew into the lumpy thing and wiggled his fingers.

It made music.

It was not like any music Kevin Spoon had ever heard.

"That's neat," he said.

"See?" Mason Mintz said.

"Where did you get that?" Kevin Spoon asked.

"It's old," Mason Mintz said. "They don't have them any more. My father had it. He gave it to me."

"What is it called?"

"I told you. Doodle flute."

"Play it some more," Kevin Spoon said.

Mason Mintz played the doodle flute some more.

"I want to get one of those," Kevin Spoon said.

"Can't," Mason Mintz said. "This is the last one there is."

Mason Mintz went away, playing his doodle flute.

The next day, Kevin Spoon saw Mason Mintz.

"Do you still have that doodle flute?"

"Yep."

"Want to sell it?"

"Nope."

"Will you sell it to me for five dollars?"

"Nope."

"Why not?"

"Don't want to."

"I'll give you ten dollars for it," Kevin Spoon said.

"No thanks," Mason Mintz said.

"Hey! You want my waterproof watch?" Kevin Spoon asked Mason Mintz.

"For free?" Mason Mintz asked.

"For the doodle flute," Kevin Spoon said.

"Nope," Mason Mintz said.

"How about my running shoes?"

"Sorry."

"My running shoes *and* my waterproof watch?"

"No can do."

"You want my guppies?"

"No."

"My stereo?"

"No."

"*All* my stuff?"

"Nix."

"Why not? Why don't you? Why don't you want all my stuff?" Kevin Spoon asked.

"I just don't," Mason Mintz said.

And he went away, playing his doodle flute, wearing his plaid hat.

Kevin Spoon told his parents, "I want a doodle flute."

"A flute?"

"A doodle flute."

After they had their pizza, Kevin went with his father.

They went to the music store.

"Do you have a doodle flute?" Kevin asked the man in the store.

"We have flutes, but no doodle flutes."

"How about a guitar?" Kevin's father asked.

"I want a doodle flute," Kevin said.

"Here's an electronic keyboard," Kevin's father said. "You want this?"

"I want a doodle flute," Kevin said.

"A piano?"

"No."

"A horn?"

"No."

"A harp?"

"No."

"Drums?"

"No."

"Whistles, fiddles, clarinets?"

"No."

"Anything at all?"

"No. I want a doodle flute."

Kevin and his father drove home.

"They didn't have a doodle flute," Kevin told his mother.

The next day, Mason Mintz came down the alley.

"I want your doodle flute," Kevin Spoon said.

"I know you do," Mason Mintz said.

"I offered you all my stuff for it."

"You did."

"But you won't trade."

"I won't."

"And you won't sell it for money."

"That's right."

"If I asked you to give it to me, would you?"

"Ask me and see."

"Mason Mintz, will you give me the doodle flute?"

"Yes."

"You will?"

"Sure."

Mason Mintz gave Kevin Spoon the doodle flute.

"I don't understand," Kevin Spoon said.

"What don't you understand?" Mason Mintz asked.

"Why are you giving me this? You wouldn't trade for all my stuff."

"That's just the kind of guy I am," Mason Mintz said, and walked away up the alley, wearing his plaid hat.

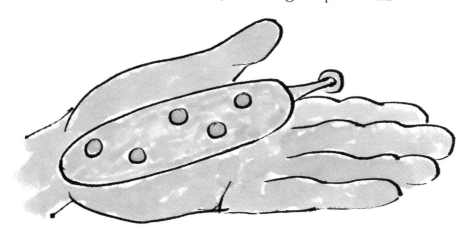

Kevin Spoon blew into
the doodle flute.
It sounded lousy.
"Rats!" Kevin Spoon said.
"I don't know how to play this."

He walked up the alley to Mason Mintz's house.

Mason Mintz was in the back yard.

He was watering the pumpkins.

"Hey!" Kevin Spoon said.

"Ho!" Mason Mintz said.

"Teach me to play this thing."

"I can't do that," Mason Mintz said.

"Why not?" Kevin Spoon asked.

"I have given up playing the doodle flute."

"Why? Why have you given up playing the doodle flute?"

"Because I don't own one," Mason Mintz said. "What's the point of being a doodle flute player if you haven't got a doodle flute?"

"But I have one," Kevin Spoon said.

"Yes, you have," Mason Mintz said.

"But I can't play it," Kevin Spoon said.

"No, you can't," Mason Mintz said.

"And you won't teach me," Kevin Spoon said.

"Sorry," Mason Mintz said. "That's just the kind of guy I am."

Kevin Spoon thought.

"If you had a doodle flute," Kevin Spoon said, "and I had a doodle flute, would you teach me then?"

"Yes."

"Well then," Kevin Spoon said, "what if we *both* owned the doodle flute? What if we shared it? Would you teach me to play it?"

"That would be okay," Mason Mintz said.

So Kevin Spoon sat down with Mason Mintz in his pumpkin patch, and Mason Mintz taught Kevin Spoon to play the doodle flute.